A TRICK OF LIGHT

A TRICK OF LIGHT

Barbara Corcoran

Illustrated by Lydia Dabcovich

ATHENEUM 1972 NEW YORK

For Andrea Jacqueline Dixon
and James Paige Dixon

1647836

A TRICK OF LIGHT

ONE

Cassandra pressed her face against the window of the school bus and stared miserably at the bleak New Hampshire countryside. Almost the end of March, and the granular snow was still piled up along the road.

Most of the students had already been let off the bus; only half a dozen boys were left, horsing around in the back and making a lot of racket. Her twin brother Paige was one of them, and it made her sick to see him act like that. He never used to. He was always level-headed and aloof from all that kind of stuff. Now

3

he was acting like a big booby, helping the other boys lift poor skinny little Jake Marbut up against the ceiling. Just a bunch of bullies. Jake was trying to be a good sport but his face was red.

It had been a rotten day right from the start. C in the history test—Paige of course got an A—and then there had been that static about her purple pantsuit. It was a new suit that Aunt Lynn in New York had sent her for her birthday, and it was beautiful, with a long tunic and a white standup collar and what her mother said was called a jabot all down the front. Her teacher

4

had admired it the other day and asked her where she got it. Cassandra asked her mother.

"Franklin Simon," her mother had said. And when Cassandra kept forgetting the name, she said, "Think of Benjamin Franklin and Simple Simon."

So when she wore it again today and Mrs. Adams asked her again where it came from, she said, "Simple Simon."

The whole class heard her, but they'd never have known she'd made a mistake—after all, there could be a store called Simple Simon—if Paige hadn't burst out laughing and told everybody. It was humiliating.

She and Paige, the youngest in a family of six, had always been as close as if they were one person. They had protected and defended each other against everyone, and confided things to each other that they would never tell anyone else. She couldn't understand what was happening to them now. Paige avoided her to hang around with a bunch of stupid boys, especially that dumb old Buddy Baker. And it seemed to her he betrayed her a dozen times a day.

She didn't know where to turn. Danny was the only one she could even think of talking to. But even Danny was too busy now that he was star of the high school basketball team. He had always been a loner, the one who spent his time in the woods by himself or in his room with his eye glued to a microscope. Nobody had paid any special attention to him, except the twins, who admired his knowledge of the woods and his independence; but then all at once his tall skinny body and long arms and legs had turned into an efficient machine for tossing a basketball through a hoop, and now everybody paid attention. More, probably, than he wanted. Cassandra suspected he had gone out for the team just to please their father.

Cassandra watched a cloud of cedar waxwings swirl and turn like smoke on the wind. She wished Jen were here so she could talk to her and forget her misery. But Jen got off at the first stop. Anyway she was a little bit mad at Cassandra because Cassandra had broken a promise to go over to Jen's house last Sunday and had gone skiing with Paige instead.

"All Paige has to do is say come and you come running," Jen had complained. And Cassandra couldn't argue because it was true. She'd rather do things with Paige than with anybody else.

One of the roughhousing boys stumbled and fell against Cassandra. "Watch it!" she said sharply, and pulled even closer to the window. Her mother always said to think of something nice when you felt depressed. For a moment she couldn't think of anything nice at all. Then she decided to think about English class on Wednesday. Some of them had read a scene aloud from *As You Like It*, and she had been Rosalind. That was one thing she was pretty good at, acting. She was always imagining things anyway; and acting after all was something like imagining.

After class, Mrs. Mahoney had said, "Very fine, Cassandra. You should be an actress; you have the gift."

Cassandra had felt good, because a lot of kids heard her. "Oh, I'm going to be," she had said. "I'm going to Germany to study in the theater."

Mrs. Mahoney looked surprised and said, "Germany? Why Germany?"

At the time Cassandra couldn't think why she had said that, so she'd had to spoil her moment of glory by muttering something about the theater being interesting there, and Mrs. Mahoney had laughed. Sometimes her teachers told her mother that Cassandra had such an imagination, they never knew when she was telling the truth and when she was having a flight of fancy. Once she had heard her mother say, "A flight of fancy can be truth, too."

Now, on the bus, she remembered why she had said Germany. When she brought home her copy of *As You Like It*, her mother had said that long ago she'd seen a German actress, Elizabeth Bergner, in a movie of *As You Like It*.

The bus jerked and coughed as it turned into the dirt road that would take the twins to within a quarter mile of their house. She wondered if anyone would be home. If Ophelia was home, she would be on the phone, yakking away to some boy. And if Rosalind was around, she'd be up in the attic practicing her ballet.

Their father, whom they called Poppy, would still be at the high school, where he taught math and woodworking. Once a week he had an evening class in cabinetmaking that people came to from all over the county. He made and sold early American reproductions, and the house and barn were always full of works in progress.

Their mother was the postmistress, a comforable plump woman whom they called Muth. Cassandra had run into a problem with the spelling of *Muth* when she wrote an English theme last year. The family had come up with several suggestions. *Moth* sounded like a bug, and *Mothe* didn't look right at all, so she settled for *Muth* but when Mrs. Mahoney read the theme in class, she pronounced *Muth* with a soft *th*, so it came out sounding all squashed and peculiar.

Muth would be someone you could tell your troubles to, but she was always so busy. Besides running the P.O., she had a big vegetable garden and flower garden in the summer, two goats, five sheep, a bunch of exotic fowl including two peacocks that screamed in the night (a bloody good thing, Poppy always said, that their only near neighbor was Mrs. Ames, who didn't hear too well), and the apple orchard that had come with the place; in the winter Muth braided rugs to sell, and did a million other things.

That was all there was to the household, except of course for the pets—Rosalind's cats, Ophelia's canary, all sorts of sick and wounded creatures that Danny brought home, and, best of all, Bingo, the Labrador retriever who had been the twins' constant companion since he was given to them on their fifth birthday.

So there was nobody, really, that Cassandra could tell her sorrows to except Bingo, who always listened attentively and looked at her understandingly with his warm brown eyes. Bingo was the very best friend she had, next to Paige and Danny.

Her mind came back to the bus as she heard Jake Marbut squeal with dismay. Mr. Haines, the bus driver, glanced in the rear view mirror and said, "You kids cut that out now." He always said that, and no one even heard him any more; his voice was part of the scene, like the squeak and rattle of the bus and the thump of the snow tires.

Cassandra turned around. The boys had Jake spread across the narrow aisle, his head on one seat, his feet on the other, his back sagging almost to the floor. They were laughing like maniacs, Paige the loudest of all. Suddenly Cassandra couldn't stand it. She scrambled into the aisle and raised both hands to the roof to keep

9

her balance. Her open coat swung back.

"Hey!" She used her loudest, most piercing voice. The boys were startled, and she saw Paige's annoyed frown. "Leave Jake Marbut alone!"

"Yah!" said Tommy Rankin derisively.

Cassandra brought one hand down in a clenched fist. She was taller than any of the boys except Paige. "The first kid that touches Jake gets clobbered."

"Oh, shut up, Cass," Paige said. But the boys were impressed. Muttering, they let Jake up. He scuttled into a rear seat, embarrassed at having been rescued by a girl.

"Who do you think you are, Cassandra Drake?" Timmy Perkins said.

"I think I'm me, that's who I am, and you'd better believe it."

"Yah," Tommy said again. He began to drum with his boot heels on the seat in front of him.

"Cut that out," Mr. Haines said.

All the boys except Paige were drumming with their heels now. Paige flopped into a seat by himself and stared morosely out the window. Cassandra looked in despair at his long handsome face, his dark hair hanging over his eyes. Half of her own self, her very being, sat there angrily looking out the window and there was no way to reach him. She went up to the front of the bus and waited by the door until Mr. Haines pulled up at their stop.

"Watch yourself, Cass," he said, with his best attempt at wit. He pulled the lever that opened the door.

"So long," Cassandra said, trying to sound bright and with it. "So long, dear old Mr. Haines." She jumped down and set off at a brisk walk across the meadow, the short cut to their house. Paige would be somewhere behind her but she wasn't about to look back.

TWO

Cassandra automatically checked out the animals as she came from the meadow into the big back yard of the Drakes' rambling 19th century farmhouse. The sheep were spread out over the hill, looking for bare patches in the snow. The goats were in the enclosure where they had to be kept so they wouldn't eat

13

the clothes off the clothesline, and all the other things that appealed to them. The peacocks were strutting around as if they owned the farm. She could see the bantam rooster and the Polish chickens, pecking around near the henhouse, with the Rhode Island Reds. In the barn, next to a half-finished hutch table, a mourning dove perched on the snowmobile that belonged to Ronald, their oldest brother, who was away at college.

The tabby cat named Persephone loped up to have her ears scratched. "Where's Bingo?" Cassandra said to the cat. Bingo almost always was waiting for them when they got home from school. "Maybe he went for a jaunt in the woods and forgot what time it was." She looked off toward the woods at the north end of their property but there was no sign of the dog. Beyond the woods the White Mountains lifted snowy peaks into the gray sky. Only Chocorua's granite face was clear of snow, too precipitous to hold it long. In the far distance she could just make out the haze that was the Presidentials.

She looked into the horse stall nearest the door to see if the fox kits Danny had found were all right. There were five of them, left orphaned when some fool had shot the mother. They were asleep now, dark brown balls of fluff, snuggled up together on an old

14

plaid bathrobe of Ronald's, in a packing crate. Danny fed them milk with a medicine dropper.

As she went up the walk to the kitchen, Paige came angling across the front lawn. He had come the long way around, up the road—so he wouldn't have to walk with me, she thought. She knocked the snow off her boots and went into the back hall, where all sorts of winter coats and pants, fishing clothes, overshoes, snowshoes, and skis, were crammed in with fishing tackle, ski poles, hockey sticks. She hung up her parka and smoothed down her jabot and went into the kitchen, heading for the refrigerator. After school was always the hungriest time.

She decided to make what was known in the family as a Cass sandwich. It had no specific requirements except that it should be at least three layers high, part meat and part something different, like marshmallow fluff. She was putting the salami and lettuce on the bottom layer, and getting ready to spread peanut butter and raspberry jam on the second layer, when Paige came into the kitchen. She braced herself for unpleasantness.

But he only glanced at her sandwich and said, "Where's Bingo?"

"How do I know?"

With exaggerated patience he said, "I thought you

15

might have seen him out back."

"If he was out back, he'd be in here by now."

Paige gave an elaborate shrug, as if he were coping with an impossible person, and went into the hall and up the stairs two at a time. Cassandra knew he was just as hungry as she was but he wouldn't admit it. After she left the kitchen, he'd sneak in and make himself a sandwich. She gritted her teeth. If he wanted to be like that, let him. Boys were stupid, stupid, stupid!

She took her sandwich upstairs to her room. No one else seemed to be home. As she passed Paige's room, he said, "Mrs. Ames was knocking on her window when I came by."

That was the funny part. They couldn't stop communicating with each other even when they were mad. "What'd she want?"

"I pretended I didn't see her."

"She might need something."

Mrs. Ames was an elderly shut-in, in a wheelchair. She was really very nice; Cassandra often dropped in to talk to her. She had a Ph.D. in linguistics, and she could tell you the strangest things about what you had just said. But sometimes, of course, you didn't feel like sitting and rapping with Mrs. Ames about Indo-European roots and all. Still, Cassandra felt responsible for her, especially during the day when Mr. Ames was in town at the bank. "I'll go over and see what she wants."

She went into her room and sat down with her sandwich in front of her mirror. People looked so awful when they ate. She was trying to work out a method of chewing that wouldn't be so repulsive. It wasn't easy though. As she began to unbutton her tunic, to change into after-school clothes, the phone rang. She started to go and answer it, but then she stopped. It would be one of Paige's friends, probably Buddy Baker. Paige and Buddy Baker had gotten very chummy.

The phone rang again.

"Hey!" Paige's voice sounded muffled. "Answer the phone."

"Answer it yourself. It will be one of your gang." She put all of her irony into the word *gang*. All their lives they had agreed that groups and gangs were for the birds. Now here was Paige . . .

Again the phone rang.

"Answer it!"

"Answer it yourself."

"I can't. My zipper's stuck."

She started to yell, "What zipper?" but thought better of it. It might be his pants zipper, and suddenly boys' pants had become something Nice Young

Ladies didn't talk about. At least that was the word they got from ancient Mrs. Evans, who taught a course called Social Relationships, which Poppy said was the Gibson Girls' version of Sex Education. Mrs. Evans said that Nice Young Ladies exercised restraint about such matters as boys' clothing and. . . . The phone whirred again. "Oh, the hell with it," she muttered, and went out into the hall to answer it on the extension. It was Mrs. Ames.

"Cassandra dear, I tried to get Paige's attention when he went by," she said. "I wanted to tell you children—"

"I guess he didn't hear you." Cassandra defended Paige from habit. "Are you all right, Mrs. Ames?"

"Yes, dear, I'm fine, but something has happened—"

"What happened?" Cassandra felt her chest tighten. To Muth? To Poppy? To one of the others?

"I hate to have to tell you this, Cass. A car hit Bingo."

"Oh, no!"

"It didn't kill him but it hurt him badly, I'm afraid. There's blood in the road. I looked through my binoculars—"

"Mrs. Ames, where is he?"

"The car sped away without even stopping. I

18

couldn't get the license number—"

"Where is he, Mrs. Ames?" She felt as if she might faint. Bingo, Bingo. . . .

"He got up after a minute and sort of stumbled off up the road. I would have called the police, Cassandra, but I knew you'd be home in a few minutes. I hope I did the right thing."

"Yes. Thank you." Cassandra hung up and stared at the phone.

"Was it Buddy?" Paige came out of his room in his scruffy blue jeans and the heavy blue sweatshirt that zipped up the front.

"No. It was Mrs. Ames."

"Oh. She okay?"

Cassandra looked at him. "Bingo's been hurt." She saw his face go white. She hated to tell him, but she repeated what Mrs. Ames had said.

He started to run down the stairs.

"Wait for me," she said.

He turned and yelled at her, all his worry concentrated in an attack on her. "You can't hunt for a wounded dog in a *purple pantsuit!*" He disappeared and she heard him rummaging around in the back hall, and then the slam of the door.

She raced back into her room and in time that was fast even for her, she changed into ski pants, sweater, heavy socks and boots. She grabbed her parka off the hook in the hall and ran outside.

Paige was already far up the road, going at a steady jog. The biggest of their collection of sleds, a long Flexible Flyer, was propped up by the steps. She grabbed the rope and sped off after Paige. If Bingo was hurt, they'd need something to bring him home on. He was a big dog.

She saw the puddle of blood in the road, crusted over now. Her stomach turned over. If anything bad happened to Bingo . . . he was so much a part of Paige and her, it was impossible to think of anything happening to him, because that would mean everything would fall apart. He had to be all right.

Drops of blood made a trail on the hard-packed snow. She knew she ought to do something sensible, like call the vet or her father, but there was Paige, getting smaller in the distance. And somewhere Bingo was wounded, needing them. She ran down the road, pulling the long sled behind her.

The runners of the sled grated whenever they hit bare patches of ground. She would jerk it impatiently and keep going. She was running, but Paige kept his distance ahead of her. The least he could do was wait for her. She was sure he knew she was coming.

She stopped and cupped her mouth with her hands.

"Paige!" He didn't even slow down. "Paige, wait." She kicked at a frozen hummock of grass. "Wait, damn it." She started up again, jerking the sled along. A cold east wind had come up, and the sky was overcast. On both sides of the road the woods looked dark and gloomy, snow piled up against their trunks. Sometimes it was almost summer before that old hard snow melted. Where could Bingo be heading? Every few feet there were drops of blood. She hoped he wasn't suffering too much. He must be in pain, though, or he wouldn't have run away from them like that. Danny said when animals were sick or hurt, they liked to go off by themselves. She looked at her watch. If Dr. Kenneth had left the office by the time they got Bingo home, they'd call his house. He'd come over; he was good about that. And the Drakes, with all their assortment of animals, were among his best customers. He was a good vet; he'd fix Bingo up. Once when Alfred, the Siamese tomcat, had been in a terrible fight and staggered home half dead, Dr. Kenneth had stayed up all night with him and pulled him through. She tried to think about Alfred now, to keep her mind off Bingo. Alf had looked really weird after that experience, with two legs in casts, one ear chewed down to a nub, and part of his tail gone, not to mention missing chunks of his coat. But he had lived on for another three years,

21

until a car hit him. Darn cars! She'd like to get them all taken off the road. Let people ride bikes. When she was older, she was going to form a league against the internal combustion engine.

Ahead of her Paige stopped and peered down at the ground, then turned off onto an old road that nobody used any more. She and Paige knew that road well; it went to a lead mine abandoned years ago. On her desk at home she had a big ball of lead that Paige had found at the mine and given to her for a paperweight. It was very heavy and really rather ugly, but she treasured it.

The picture of her bedroom rose up in her mind— a warm, comfortable, disorderly room, with a big desk made from a door and two sawhorses; a four-poster bed she had recently inherited from Rosalind, who thought it was decadent; and the Beatrix Potter prints that she kept on her walls, although Ophelia said they were for babies. She wished she were lying on her bed right now in her old faded blue terrycloth robe, with Bingo sprawled on the rug beside the bed. From downstairs where Muth would be be fixing dinner, there would come marvelous smells of cooking. . . . She thought of the sandwich on her bureau, half-eaten, and wished she had brought it.

Danny would be in his room with the door shut,

playing his new album of the song of the whales. Poppy would come in, put on his fleece-lined slippers and slump into his leather chair with a can of beer and a big sigh and a "What's for dinner, love?"

Up in the attic where Poppy had built a practice bar and put in a big mirror, Rosalind would be rehearsing her ballet steps with frowning concentration, to the worn Swan Lake record on the old record player Ronald had discarded long ago.

And Ophelia would be on the phone. Or practicing the viola in her room. Although she had such a passion for rock that Danny called her "the groupie," she also played the viola, quite well, in the school orchestra. Actually Ophelia might turn out all right when she got through the eyeshadow and groovy boys stage.

Just ahead of her, Paige came to a stop. He had reached the mine site, and he was whistling for Bingo. Cassandra looked up at the rickety remains of the chutes, just barely hanging together, like shadows against the snow and the trees. Mining lead seemed like an unromantic business, but there was something eerie and mysterious about the structure that had been left, perhaps only because of its age.

"Why didn't you wait up for me?" Cassandra said. "I yelled and yelled at you. After all, Bingo is my dog too, you know."

He gave her a faraway look, as if he wasn't thinking about her at all. "I've lost the trail."

She looked back and realized there were no spots of blood. She hadn't noticed because she had just been following Paige and thinking her thoughts.

He looked all around, examining the brush on both sides of the road. "If he was heading for some place familiar, it could have been here—"

"Or it could have been any place at all. He's been all over this area a million times." When she saw his worried look, she was sorry she had snapped at him.

He went over to a faintly defined path that led into the woods. "And maybe he wouldn't even care about familiar or not." He hunkered down and stared at the hard-grained snow. "Darned snow's so icy, it doesn't show any tracks."

"At least he's stopped bleeding."

"I don't know if that's good or bad." He leaned against a tree, discouraged. "I don't know which way to go."

Cassandra glanced at the sky. The heavy clouds would bring early darkness. Already the light was fading. "Maybe we ought to go home and wait till morning."

He shook his head. "No. You can go home if you want to. I'm staying till I find him."

25

"I'm not going if you don't."

"Then let's get moving. We'll just have to search every place, I guess." He stood in the road indecisively a moment longer, whistled and called Bingo. Both of them strained to hear some answering bark, but there was no sound in the dark snowy woods.

"Maybe he went down the path to the camp," Cassandra said. The path, mostly unused now, led through the woods to Camp Brio, a girls' summer camp where Danny had a job looking after the horses during vacation. They had gotten to know Mrs. Carstairs, the owner, and sometimes she let them play tennis when the campers weren't using the courts. When camp was closed, the twins often went over there and wandered around the many trails, or had a picnic on the big porch of the recreation building that jutted out over the lake.

"All right, let's hit for camp." Paige plunged into the thick scrub oak, following the almost invisible path. He stopped abruptly as a whitetail doe rose up out of the brush and crossed in front of them with a bound. They watched her until she was out of sight. She looked ragged, her bluish winter coat beginning to shed, but even so, Cassandra thought, there was nothing so beautiful as a deer.

Paige started on again, but Cassandra was having

26

trouble with the sled, which kept catching on bushes and banging into trees. She thought about leaving it, but then, they didn't know how far they might have to carry Bingo, and he really was heavy. The sled might mean life or death for him. She struggled on, trying to ease it through the woods. For the moment, Paige was out of sight. She wished he would help her with the sled but she knew that wasn't fair; she was the one who had brought it. Anyway, he was so worried, he might not even have noticed she had it. He always worried more than she did. She was not going to despair unless she really had to; Bingo had survived all sorts of things in his lifetime. He'd be all right.

Paige loomed up in front of her at a turn in the path where he had waited for her. In a few minutes they would be able to see the lake. "That's a nuisance," he said, looking at the sled.

Thinking he was criticizing her, she said, "Well, we can't just carry him out."

He winced. "I know. It was a good idea." He looked at it thoughtfully for a moment. Then, pulling it loose from the bushes where it had caught, he hoisted it up, runners out, against his back and hooked his arms under the ends of the steering bar.

Cassandra was sorry again for having been so crabby. "You don't have to carry it. It was my idea."

27

He gave her a small grin. "Us men gotta bear the burden."

"Better not let Mary Evans hear you say that." Mary Evans was Ophelia's women's lib friend. Paige chuckled and Cassandra felt good that they were friends again.

It was slow going through the dense woods as the light failed. The branches of white pines were still bent with snow but here and there a gaunt pitch pine thrust up its asymmetrical form into the dark sky.

Both of them tried to watch for signs of Bingo, and every few minutes they called but it was hard to see much, and there was no answering bark.

When they reached the place where the path intersected the snow-covered road that led to the camp, Paige gave a shout.

"What is it?"

He dropped the sled and got down on his knees. "A track!"

Cassandra's heart jumped. She got down beside him. There was a track, all right, one paw print that had broken through the crust of snow. "Do you think it's Bing's?"

He studied it. "Can't tell. When it breaks the snow like that, it kind of loses shape. It looks big, though, and there aren't too many big animals around here."

"Deer?"

"I don't think so. A deer track would be deeper, and more pointed and together. There's no scat anywhere." He straightened up and looked at Cassandra with the first sign of cautious hope. "So it could be Bing though I'm not saying it is."

"I'll bet he headed for camp."

"Let's go." He ran down the road toward camp, pulling the sled behind him and calling.

Cassandra came more slowly, trying to scan both sides of the road. There was only that one print. The snow in the road was packed so hard that not even the runners of the sled left a track. So they couldn't really tell if Bingo had gone on to camp or had stopped and turned off, maybe toward Moore's Pond or somewhere else. She looked for trampled brush but she didn't see any. The scrub oak had grown up thick and stiff in the aftermath of a forest fire a dozen years before that had destroyed the pines. Mrs. Carstairs had started a pine-planting program; every summer the girls set out white pine seedlings. The earliest of these had already grown to three or four feet, their five-needled clusters heaped now with tiny mounds of snow. It didn't look like a good place for a hurt dog to seek refuge so maybe he really had headed for camp. Maybe in just a few minutes now, they would all three be together again, just like old times. She ran down the road, humming the song Poppy used to sing after they got Bingo:

"B-i-n-g, O-go, Bingo, B-i-n-g, O-go, Bingo,
  B-i-n-g, O-go, Bingo, down on the Bingo farm."

THREE

When they came up over the hump of the hill, they could see part of the camp. Here the pines, untouched by the fire, were tall. Ahead of them was the little log cabin called the Store, where the girls got their mail and bought raisins and graham crackers and little cartons of milk. Mrs. Carstairs was of the opinion that candy made the teeth fall out, so the only sweets the girls got were those sent them by their parents, which, Danny said, they sometimes sold to their friends at black market prices.

Behind the Store were the tennis courts, and the

path that led around the courts to the Men's Tent, where Danny and the other male workers lived. The Men's Tent was always the prime target of raids by the girls on the rare nights when most of the counselors were away at a movie. In Danny's opinion, Mrs. Carstairs deliberately set up those nights of anarchy to prevent the explosion of mischief on a larger scale. Most of the time she rode the camp with a tight rein.

Past the Cottage where Mrs. Carstairs lived during the camp season, on the other side of the road and over the dip of the land as it sloped down toward the lake, Cassandra could see the green shingled roof of the Inn.

Paige had paused to scan the area in front of him. It was almost dark, and Cassandra wondered again if they ought not to be starting home. It was no use looking for Bingo in the dark. But at once her mind rejected the idea of just leaving him somewhere all night. If they stayed out overnight, they could start to search as soon as it was light. Muth and Poppy might worry a little, but they would know from Mrs. Ames about Bingo and they would realize that the twins were hunting for him. Danny would reassure them. She could hear him saying, "Those kids are self-reliant. I taught them myself. Quit worrying." They would probably worry a little but not too much. One of the nice things about them was that they trusted their children.

If only she'd thought to bring some food. She felt as if her stomach had caved in altogether. It wouldn't have taken a minute to grab some cans of sardines and some cheese or something. Maybe they weren't as smart as Danny thought they were. He was great for living off the land and he had taught the twins, especially Paige, to recognize wild foods, so probably they wouldn't starve. Although it wasn't so simple in the winter, and anyway the thought of a tasty dinner of rose hips and squirrel stew made her gag. She had never been all that crazy about wild food although, of course, it was a comfort to know you could keep from starving to death at least. She wondered if Paige had any matches.

When she caught up with him, he said, "I hope there's something to eat left in the Inn." He so often was thinking what she was thinking, it never surprised her.

"Are you going to break in?"

"Yeah. We just about have to. We can pay Mrs. Carstairs back, or replace whatever we take. She wouldn't want us to starve to death over a moral scruple." He paused. "Or would she?"

"Well, I'm not sure."

33

"I could find some wild stuff but it will really be dark in a few minutes. Cold, too." He looked at her. "Maybe you ought to go home."

"I'm not going until you do. I want to find Bingo."

"All right." He trotted down the hill, the sled nipping at his heels.

When he came to the Inn, he sat down on the broad steps to think. Behind him the big dining room, screened in summer, was boarded up, and there were boards over the windows of the big kitchen and the serving room. The counselors' room was around in the back.

Cassandra sat down beside him. She was tired. It was a long hike to the camp, and they had come the longest way. The evening chill closed in around them, making them shiver. The wind had died down some but there was still enough to make the pines rustle.

The ground in front of the steps was bare, and Cassandra noticed a lot of tiny bird tracks from an early thaw, making a design like the filigree on Muth's silver service. "What were all those birds doing here?"

Paige leaned over and picked up a sunflower seed. "Danny must have been up here feeding them."

She hadn't even noticed the seed. It exasperated her that Paige and Danny always saw so much more than she did. She leaned back, thinking about Mrs. Carstairs, who was also a great noticer. "Remember the

34

time Danny broke the water cooler?" she said, but Paige only nodded absently. She knew he was thinking about what to do next. She ought to be thinking too but sometimes you had to rest your mind for a minute.

Danny always said, "Underneath that tough exterior Mrs. Carstairs has a heart of stone." She was very strict with the boys who worked for her, and she wanted things done her way. Sometimes Danny did them his way, and then they clashed. Once, putting the big chunk of ice into the water cooler, his way, he

dropped it and broke the cooler. "She cussed me out for twenty minutes without taking a breath," he told them later, "but after that, we got along better."

"She was mean to bawl you out," Cassandra had said. "It was only an accident."

"Oh, no. She had to do it. I wouldn't have respected her if she hadn't."

Boys were funny. Cassandra was sure she'd much rather be loved than respected. "Do you respect me?" she asked Paige.

He looked bewildered by such a question at such a time. "Respect you? What's that got to do with anything?"

"I just wondered. Do you?" She was sorry she'd asked; it was a dumb question.

He shrugged. "I guess so. I respect myself so I must respect you."

She was pleased, not so much that he respected her as that he had acknowledged that they were still two halves of one whole. She felt better than she had in weeks.

But then he had to look at his watch and say, "Buddy will be wondering where I am. We were going to do some yakking on the ham set after school." And her moment of happiness disappeared. Damned old Buddy Baker. He was always off with Buddy Baker. When they weren't fooling around with Buddy's short-wave set, they were tossing a football around. In Cassandra's opinion anyone who played football in the spring had no sense of the fitness of things.

"I guess he'll survive," she said sharply.

Paige's face clouded. "Why are you so nasty?"

"Because boys are so stupid."

He groaned. "Turn the record over, will you? I've heard that side." He got up, went down the stone steps, and started down the path to the lake.

"Where are you going?" Sometimes when he got mad and walked away, she got the feeling he might never come back.

"I want to look around the lake before it's too dark."

"I'll go with you."

"No, you stay here in case Bing shows up. No sense both of us being in the same place."

She started down the steps after him just the same. She didn't want to stay there in the dark alone; it was spooky. She tried to hurry but whoever had made the steps had put them too close together for her long legs. Near the bottom her foot skidded off the worn rock and she fell. She made a grab for Paige to break her fall, missed him, and fell headlong on the frozen ground.

"Are you all right?" He helped her up. "Man, you went down with a crash."

She felt shaken up, her head hurt, and her left knee

had a shooting pain. "I think I'm okay. Those stupid steps." She took a few steps gingerly to test the knee. "I banged my knee but I guess it's still working."

"You cut your cheek." He fished a handkerchief out of his parka and held it to her face. They looked at the drops of blood on it. "Listen, you better sit down or something."

"I'm all right." But she let him lead her back up the steps.

"I'll stay here if you want."

"No." She could be generous too, kind and gracious and a joy to have for a sister, as he would see. "You go search. I'll wait here."

"Well, whistle if you need me. I won't be far away."

"Right." She watched him trot down the path that led to the lake and then start around the shore, away from the boat house. She sighed and leaned her head against the Inn door, looking down to the lake. In front of her, past the wide lawn, stretched the frozen lake. The ice was beginning to break up at the shoreline, and she could hear the faint lap of the water. About a half mile out was the dark blur of Loon Island, where the older girls swam in summer and sometimes camped out overnight. The lake went on for another three miles to the little village at the end, which she couldn't see in the dark. Danny said the poet e.e. cummings used to live in a tree house on the eastern shore of the lake, and he was a grown man at the time. It would be nice to have enough nerve to do things like that when you were grown up—live in a tree house and spell your name with little letters and write poems. She didn't really want to write poems, but she liked to recite them.

She got up and walked down to the boat house. Looking in the dusty window, she could see the pale blur of the dock, stacked on its side, and the stacked-up canoes and the two rowboats. She walked down the beach a little way, in the opposite direction from the way Paige had gone. She wished she could be the one to find Bingo. She couldn't bear to have him out there in the woods alone and hurt. She kept seeing him in her mind, his lovely noble head with its floppy ears and long face. He was too big to get into her lap but he liked to put his front paws in her lap and push his head against her. She would smooth down his short coat. Outdoors he played with them like a puppy, even now, running like the wind and chasing them around the meadow where the sheep grazed. Even Muth, who was not a terribly doggy person, loved him. Cassandra stopped in a clump of white birches where someone had built a seat between two trees. She sat down. Her head ached, and she felt like crying her eyes out for Bingo. If anything happened to him. . . . But they simply would not let it.

People had carved their initials into the soft white bark of the tree. That made her mad. You could kill a birch that way, quick as anything. Stupid city girls.

Slowly she walked back to the Inn, thinking she would wait for Paige but then she changed her mind and took the path toward the point where the recreation building was. She passed the platforms where the girls' tents were in the summer. Mrs. Carstairs didn't believe in city conveniences like bungalows and modern plumbing. The girls lived three campers and a counselor to a tent, with one mirror and one dressing table. They brought water in pitchers from the facility down behind the tent area, where there were eight chemical toilets and a long sink with water piped from the lake. Sometimes on a Sunday morning Cassandra had seen the girls standing waist deep in the lake washing their hair, suds piled up on their heads like Martha Washington's wig.

At the flagpole there was a flight of steps down, logs built into the earth, leading to the recreation house. She went down them, holding onto the railing, and out onto the wide porch that hung over the lake and the path that Paige had taken. From here she could see him when he came back. She wished he would hurry; she didn't like being alone. When she was alone with nothing to do, she started to think, and in her opinion thinking was a very uncomfortable pastime. Like now, it got harder and harder to persuade herself that Bingo was all right. In some way that she didn't want to consider, she felt uneasy not only about Bingo but about Paige and herself, as if somehow Bingo held them together, held their childhood and their closeness to each other between his big friendly paws. It was a crazy idea, and she firmly put it out of her mind.

Cassandra wished she were more like Rosalind. She doubted if Roz ever wasted much time thinking about anything but her dancing. Cassandra envied the dedicated. Roz had started dancing as soon as she could walk, and for five years now she had gone to Center Ossipee every week for ballet lessons from Miss Winslow, who was terribly old but who used to dance with the Ballet Russe de Monte Carlo. Miss Winslow said Rosalind was going to be a great ballerina, and they all believed it. Muth and Poppy were thinking of letting her go to live with Aunt Lynn next year and study ballet full time. Aunt Lynn knew Mr. Balanchine, who was a great choreographer. Cassandra sighed. Think of being able to drop out of school at the end of your sophomore year! Some people had all the luck. But Roz deserved it. Except for being kind of remote, she was a very nice sister.

Cassandra leaned over the balcony at the sound of a twig cracking. "Paige?" There was no answer. She felt a little nervous. Were the bears out of hibernation yet? Probably, after that thaw early in the month. She'd never heard of a bear bothering anyone around there; mostly you didn't even see them. Still, she'd just as soon not run into one in the dark. "Paige?"

This time he answered. "Yo."

She was relieved. "Hey, I'm up here on the porch."

He scrambled up the steep bank.

"Did you see anything?"

"No, nothing." They looked at each other for a second and then looked away, not wanting to acknowledge the worry they both felt. "Well, if we're going to spend the night, we need some shelter." He tried the barred door, but it wouldn't budge. He got out his big jackknife and began to pry at the board that covered the window. It took a while but he finally got it loose. He aimed the knife handle at the lower corner of the window pane and shut his eyes. "Mrs. Carstairs, forgive me, I know not what I do." His hand moved sharply downward and there was the sound of splintering glass. Cassandra wondered what the penalty was for breaking and entering.

Paige carefully removed enough glass so he could get his hand inside to reach the latch and in a few seconds he had the window open. It was a tight squeeze, but they got in.

It was dark and airless inside the big building.

Cassandra shrieked as a bat flapped past her head. Paige opened the two halves of the Dutch door, and the bat flew out.

"I wish I had a flashlight." He struck a match and held it high, to see. Firewood was stacked up neatly beside the huge fieldstone fireplace, and there was a pile of kindling. "Thank God—wood. Listen, do you want to lay a fire while I see if I can find any food up at the Inn?"

"Sure. I hope you find some. I'm perishing from hunger."

"Me too." He handed her the matches. "I'll try to hurry."

After he was gone, she laid some kindling carefully and then crossed two smaller logs on top of it, kneeling on the cold hearth. She thought of the Campfire Girls' line, "kneel always, when you light a fire." She liked that; it made her think of fire as some kind of wild pagan god, although she supposed that really wasn't what the Campfire Girls had in mind.

She stood up to look at her arrangement. She couldn't see too well in the dark building, even with the door open, but she hoped the fire would be a good one. She had the reputation of making the best fires in the family. She added one more branch bristly with pine needles, struck a match and tossed it onto the needles. They blazed up in a beautiful orange flame,

43

and then the dry kindling began to crackle.

She coughed. The fire was smoking. Could she have built it too far to the front? Was it possible that the big chimney wasn't drawing right? Then she remembered. The cap on the chimney. She had watched Danny last fall when he fitted tin caps on all the chimneys to keep the squirrels out. Frantically she tried to stamp out the fire, but it was burning too well. Smoke was thickening in the room. What had she done! The chimney would overheat, the place would burn down.

She ran outside. She would have to get up on the roof and get that tin cap off the chimney before it was too late. There was no possibility of reaching the roof from the porch without a ladder and she didn't dare wait for Paige to boost her up. She yelled for him, but she knew he wouldn't hear her.

There was just one chance. If she could get up on the slope of the hill that bordered the fourth wall, she might be able to jump across the space between building and hill, and land on the roof. If she fell into the dug-out area between the hill and the building, it wouldn't be so good . . . but there wasn't time to worry about ifs.

She scrambled diagonally from the steps up and across the lower part of the hill until she was even with the roof. She figured the distance she'd have to jump, climbed the hill a little higher to get a running start, ran quickly down the slope, held her breath and jumped. She made it. But the roof was icy and she felt herself start to slide back. She lay flat on her stomach, willing herself to stick to the roof, grabbing the curled ends of loose shingles with her fingers and trying to dig in with her toes. It felt like Ronald's description of climbing the granite face of a mountain. She wished she had a rope.

Once she managed to stop sliding, she was able to start inching slowly up, bending one knee a little at a time and cautiously moving one foot, then the other, humping forward. She fought the sense of urgency that made her want to hurry. A careless step would send her flying off the roof, and the building would burn down.

Several times she slipped back a few inches but finally, her fingers trembling, and her breathing so loud it sounded like sobbing, she clutched the cold stones of the chimney and pulled herself up to a standing position. She got one arm part way around the chimney to keep from falling, and with the other hand she removed the big rock that held the tin cover in place. It was heavy, and she had to release her other hand to put the rock down on the ridge where it wouldn't roll off. It took both hands, too, to pull off the snug-fitting cover. She hooked an ankle around the corner of the chimney and prayed that the cover wouldn't fly off suddenly and send her reeling backward.

At first she couldn't budge it, but then she felt one side give a little, and she increased pressure on the other side, the way Paige had showed her to take the tight lid off the coffee canister at home. She could hardly believe it when it came off at last. In seconds she smelled the smoke that had built up inside the chimney. She slid down to a sitting position, her back to the chimney, weak with relief. Wow! would Paige ever laugh at her for being such a dum-dum, starting a fire with the chimney blocked up. Maybe if she got down before he came back, he'd never know the difference.

She slid down the roof sitting down, going much faster than she had come up, but trying not to go so fast that she wouldn't be able to stop. Just before she got to the edge she managed to get on her feet. She ran the last few steps, hoping she wouldn't slip, and took a wide jump for the hill. She landed face down in a clump of blueberry bushes.

Scratched, dirty, cold and stiff, she hurried back inside, bringing the cover with her so she'd remember to put it back in the morning. Paige had not come back. She tried to fan the smoke out of the door with her hands. The mantel was hot and the stones had blackened in the front. It had been a narrow escape all right.

She added some more logs and stood in front of the fire to get warm. Over the mantel, in the face of the big chimney, there was a bronze plaque in memory of a girl who had died at camp ten years ago. Cassandra knew it by heart because she always looked at it when she was there. Harriet Johnson, it said, and under her name, the dates of her birth and death. She had lived for sixteen and a half years. Below the dates were the words, "A child of God, she walks in light." It haunted Cassandra to think of a girl coming to camp, perfectly healthy and happy, and then all of a sudden she was dead, and all you could see of her was a plaque over a fireplace, and probably a tombstone somewhere. She had asked Danny what the girl died of; he thought it was spinal meningitis but he wasn't sure and he said not to ask Mrs. Carstairs because she got so upset about it. The girl had been coming to camp for four years and she'd been an honor girl every year. Everybody had liked her.

"Good luck, Harriet Johnson, wherever you are," Cassandra said. "I hope you don't mind too much being dead."

She heard Paige coming down the steps.

"Yo," he said. "I come bearing gifts." He dumped an armful of things on the bench in front of the

49

piano. "And don't think it was easy. Hey, it's smoky in here." He peered into the fireplace. "Is there a damper or something?"

"Well," Cassandra said innocently, "where there's smoke, there's fire."

"Oh, funny. Well, it doesn't seem to be coming out now. I suppose you fixed whatever it was with your magic wand. Hey, look what I brought. But man, I had to hunt like mad. At first I thought there was nothing, just nothing. That Carstairs is like compulsively neat. But . . ha! . . she overlooked a couple of little faraway corners." He held up an institutional-sized can of peanut butter. "And this. . . ." A regular-sized can of beef stew.

"Beautiful. Do we put the peanut butter on the stew?"

"Listen, be grateful."

"I'll be the grateful dead if I don't get something to eat. Can opener?" She took the one he opened up for her on his knife, and pried at the can. "I could eat the tin."

He had brought two frying pans and a kettle for the stew.

"Why the frying pans?"

"For the piece of resistance." He held up a cellophane bag of popping corn. "Uncle Paige is going to pop up a storm. Save a little grease off the top of the stew for the pan."

"Yecch!"

"Well, it'll keep the corn from sticking, if I shake like mad the whole time."

The prospect of food, the rise in Paige's spirits, and the warmth of the fire made Cassandra feel euphoric. She decided to tell Paige about the chimney. She made it sound as funny as she could.

When she finished, he looked at her a moment. Then he said, "Good thinking, old twin. You're all right."

She felt happy. He hadn't been this nice to her in weeks. "Not only good thinking, boy," she said, "also clever foot work."

"Right. Very clever footwork." He chuckled. "I wish I'd seen you."

"Let's don't forget to put the thing back before we leave or the red squirrels will get in here and tear everything up, and Mrs. Carstairs will chew Danny out."

He brought out two spoons he had found, and when the stew was hot, they took turns eating it from the kettle, burning their tongues in their haste. Cassandra thought it was the very best stew she had ever eaten.

When it was gone, they ate peanut butter straight from the can. Paige poured some corn into one frying pan, covered it with the other, and shook the whole thing furiously over the fire. Soon the popping corn was pinging against the top pan. He popped a huge amount, and they sat on the floor, staring dreamily into the fire and eating the unsalted, unbuttered popcorn.

"Oh, one other little treat." Paige pulled some tea bags from his pocket. "Hold the fort." He took the empty kettle down to the lake, and came back with it clean. He had chopped a big chunk of thin ice from the lake, and now he let it melt in the kettle and come to a boil for the tea.

If it weren't for Bingo, Cassandra thought, this would be one of the nicest nights she could remember. She knew Paige had gone back to worrying; he was slumped down, his long legs stretched toward the fire, and he was eating popcorn absently. Cassandra didn't want him to lose the happy mood he'd been in. She jumped up and went over to the piano. When she pulled the bench up, opened the piano, and struck a chord, Paige groaned and said, "Oh, no." But she knew the different shades of meaning in his oh, no's, and this one didn't really mean stop.

She had taken piano lessons last year, but Poppy had made her stop because she wouldn't practice enough. She could play some things by ear, though, if they were easy and in the key of C. She started off with "Believe Me If All Those Endearing Young Charms," singing the Harvard words that Poppy had taught them: "Fair Harvard, thy sons to thy jubilee come." Then she went on to Cornell's "Here by Lake Cayuga's Waters." By the time she got to "On, on, O Harvard, on, on, O Harvard, fight right through that line," Paige had gotten up and joined in. He had a pleasant, low-pitched voice although it hadn't changed yet and sometimes broke. Cassandra loved to sing with him, but they hadn't done it for a long time. Sometimes when everyone was home, the whole family sang, with Muth playing the piano and Poppy plinking away on his banjo.

She and Paige sang "Round and Round the Old Brass Wagon," and "John Hardy." Sometimes in the flickering light, Cassandra hit the wrong notes, but she didn't pause for that. She went into Paige's favorite, "This Old Man Comes Rollin' Home."

Finally they had to stop to put more wood on the fire and eat some more popcorn. Paige maneuvered a heavy log onto the fire, brushed the dirt off his hands, and stood looking at the Johnson girl's plaque. He grew so quiet that Cassandra finally said, "It's terribly sad, isn't it."

He looked puzzled. "What is?"

"That girl. Weren't you thinking about the girl that died?"

"I was thinking about Bingo."

"Oh. I thought you were . . . you were looking at the plaque."

"Was I?" He looked at it now. "Why should I be thinking about her? She's been dead ten years."

Cassandra felt a little slice of pain under her ribs. "But she was alive. I mean she was somebody. Now she isn't."

He yawned. "You can't get all moody about everybody that ever died." He spread his parka on the floor near the fireplace and lay down. "We'd better get some sleep."

Cassandra couldn't let go of the subject. "How can you be so indifferent?"

Already he was falling asleep. "About what?"

"About somebody who was alive, right in this room . . . right where you're falling asleep. . . ."

"Oh, go to sleep." He turned over and buried his face in the hood of his parka. "Girls are funny." And he was asleep.

Cassandra was sure she wouldn't be able to sleep. The idea of sleep seemed scary; it was too much like death. I'm just going to lie here and think about Bingo and try to figure out where he might have gone. . . . But she was asleep before she finished the thought.

FOUR

DURING THE NIGHT CASSANDRA WOKE UP THINKING
she heard the wild laughter of a loon, but she must
have dreamed it. Loons went south in the winter, and
they wouldn't be stupid enough to come back while
the lake was still frozen; they lived on fish. There
were always several of them on Loon Island in the
summer, and once when she and Paige had gone out
to the island in a canoe in the spring, they had come
across some newly hatched babies paddling feebly
near the nest in one of the inlets. They were soft
downy little things, black on top and white under-

neath. Danny said sometimes the babies rode on their mothers' backs, but you didn't get close enough to an adult loon very often to see that.

She got up and put a log on the dying fire. She hoped Muth wasn't worried about them.

Paige turned over sleepily and said, "What's up?"

"Nothing. I just woke up."

He sat up and looked at his watch. "Quarter past three."

Cassandra felt wide awake. "I wish it were light." She propped her cheek on her elbow and stared at the fire.

"It won't be long." He lay back.

She didn't want him to go to sleep. It seemed as if he was always going to sleep or going off somewhere. "What do you want to be when you grow up?"

He groaned. "What a time for a question like that! Besides, you ask me every three months."

"Well, you change every three months."

"I think I'll be a radio engineer." He yawned.

"Oh, you're kidding! Just because that dumb Buddy Baker has this creepy ham set—"

"You asked me, I told you." He turned his back.

"Nobody cares about radio any more. Radio's been out for years."

"Go to sleep."

"Do you want to go through life sitting hunched

over with earphones on, saying, 'this is XR ALF 202. Come in, RX PLA 203. Come in, RX. Roger. Over and Out.' I mean do you call that living?"

Exasperated, he said, "I want to specialize in space radio."

"What's that?"

"If you weren't so ignorant—"

"So tell me and I won't be."

"Well, picking up signals in outer space. Ozma and all that."

"Ozma? The only Ozma I know is in the Wizard of Oz."

"That's what it's named for, I think. It's these huge metal discs that pick up signals from space."

"Space! Who sends them?"

His voice rose in irritation. "Nobody sends them. They're just signals."

"If there's a signal, somebody has to send it. Do you believe in little men on Venus sending you messages?"

He thumped the floor with the flat of his hand. "No, damn it. I don't know. Nobody does."

"Then why bother?"

"To *find out!* Go to sleep."

"The trouble with this world," Cassandra said, lying on her back and watching the shadows the fire made on the ceiling, "is boys thinking they know everything. Boys growing up to be big hotshot inventors. Technology, that's what's the matter. Henry Ford and all the rest of you, ruining the earth."

Paige wrapped his hood around his ears.

"Just too darned smart for their britches." But he didn't answer so she gave up. Actually she wished she hadn't started it. She seemed to be always picking a fight with him lately, when that was the last thing in the world she wanted to do. Why did she do it? She got up and walked down to the other end of the room, where a small stage filled the end of the building. She sat down on the stage. Her bones ached from lying on the cold floor. She thought of a kooky play the campers had given two summers before, called *Six Who Pass While Lentils Boil*. Insane. Just the same, she'd like to have been in it. It would be kind of great to be an actress.

Then there was the musical vespers Mrs. Carstairs had invited the Drakes to last summer. That had been really nice. The music counselor, a concert violinist, had trained the girls really well. They'd sung stuff like "God of the Mountains," which Cassandra thought was by Tschaikovsky or somebody; and they'd sung some other very nice stuff; and Mrs. Pezzati had played the violin like an angel. Just as the sun was going down, they sang "Day Is Dying in the West" and marched two by two onto the porch, and then they sang the Sevenfold Amen without an accompaniment. It was really something. Cassandra wished that she were talented. Everybody else in her family could do something. Paige sang, Roz danced, Danny played basketball, Ophelia had her viola, Muth played the piano, and Poppy the banjo. Even Ronald was on the wrestling team. But she had no claim to fame at all. No wonder Paige wanted to cut loose from her. She would just have to find something she could do well. Maybe raise peacocks; Muth said she had a way with them. But they didn't give any Nobel prizes for raising peacocks.

She was getting cold. She picked up a rope that was coiled on a corner of the stage and took it back to the fireside. They could use that in the morning when they fixed the chimney. She curled up, wrapping the parka around her legs, and went to sleep.

It seemed to be only a few minutes later that Paige was shaking her awake. "Get up. It's light. It snowed in the night."

"Snowed?" She heard the hiss of snow falling down the chimney onto the fire. "Much?"

"Not too. Maybe three or four inches."

"Gosh, isn't winter ever going to quit?" She got up and stretched to get the kinks out.

"It could be good or bad. It's covered up any old tracks, but if Bing moved around since it snowed, maybe we can pick up the trail. Let's clean up and get going."

"No breakfast?"

"Put some popcorn in your pockets. We haven't got time to mess around."

He put out the remains of the fire. "We'll come back with Danny and wash the smoke off and clean up in here." He took the cap for the chimney.

"Wait. I found a rope." She tossed it to him. "You can get up there quicker if you lasso the chimney and pull yourself up."

She went outside and watched him swing the rope. Twice he missed but on the third try the coil of the rope curled around the chimney. He pulled it taut, and took a running jump onto the roof. With the rope to pull himself along, it took him only a couple of minutes to get up to the chimney, replace the cap and the rock, and let himself down again.

He nailed a piece of wood over the broken window-pane, and they took the utensils back to the Inn. He had gotten in by jimmying the door on the counselors' room. "Danny'll have to get a better lock for this door. Anybody could break in."

They looked around the area for possible tracks, but there were none except for squirrels and chipmunks.

"I wonder which way we should go first," Paige said.

"Let's walk out to the road."

"Any reason?"

"No, except that's where we saw that one print. I just have a feeling we should go that way."

"Let's don't go all psychic about this."

"It's no more darned psychic than waiting for messages from Venus," she said, but neither of them was in the mood to quarrel. They just wanted to find Bingo.

The temperature was not very low, but there was a chill wind blowing from the east. Trees were encased in ice, and even the weeds and brush were stiff and glistening in the early sunlight.

They walked out the narrow camp road toward the county road without seeing any signs of the dog. As they climbed the last hill, past the baseball field, Cassandra stopped.

"What is it?"

"I thought I saw something move, over there in the thicket behind home plate." She shaded her eyes. "I did!" She ran toward the thicket, her heart pounding with expectation. There was something big and brown. . . . "Bingo?" No answer.

Paige was right behind her and then he overtook her. At the edge of the thicket he stopped short. "It's a deer."

Cassandra felt like crying with disappointment. She

moved in beside him to look. "It's hurt."

The deer made an effort to get up but it sank back again in the snow, trembling. It watched them with frightened eyes.

"What's wrong with it? Is it a doe?"

"No, it's a buck. See the pedicels?"

Now she could see them, the basis for the new antlers that would start to grow in a month or so.

"He must have fallen. They aren't very surefooted on snow and ice." Paige took a step toward it. "Hey, buck. Don't be scared. I'm not going to hurt you. Take it easy, old buck." He moved closer and the deer pulled back its head and shoulder, trying again to rise. "Don't worry. I want to see what's wrong."

Cassandra watched, fascinated. Paige was almost as good with animals as Danny was. She felt proud of him. She wouldn't have known what to do for the poor little buck, except to tell him she was sorry.

Very gently Paige ran his hands over the deer's hind legs. The animal turned his head to watch Paige with big liquid eyes. "Here it is." He had his hand on the right hind leg.

"Broken?"

"I don't know. It might be dislocated." He put his hand on the deer's neck. "Listen, bucko, I'm going to try to fix it, but first we got to get you up on your feet."

63

"What can I do?" Cassandra said. "Do you need a splint or anything?"

"Not if it's dislocated. You could help me get him up." As Cassandra moved cautiously closer, he said, "Don't be scared."

"I'm not scared. I don't want to scare *him*."

"He can tell we're his friends. Look, get your arms kind of around his chest if you can . . . not too close to his mouth in case he decides to take a nip. Then when I say 'heave,' we'll get him up."

"All right," Carefully she put one arm around his neck and the other across his chest. If he wanted to take a bite out of her, she thought, he had a perfect chance. But he didn't. She could feel him trembling. "Poor little deer. Don't worry. Paige will fix it."

"After he's up, kind of support him while I see what I can do. All right, one, two, three, *heave!*"

They got the buck to his feet. He tried to take a step but his injured leg gave way.

"Everybody hold steady now," Paige said.

Cassandra kept her arms around the buck, feeling the roughness of his coat. She murmured to him while Paige examined the injured leg.

"It's dislocated," he said. "Hold tight now. I'm going to try to get it back. . . ." He made a sudden strong movement with his hands. The deer jerked free from Cassandra's grip, stood still for an instant as if testing the leg, and then bounded away into the woods.

"Hey, bucko!" Paige called, laughing. "Where shall I send the bill?"

"That was wonderful," Cassandra said. "Paige, that was really impressive."

"Calling Dr. Drake . . . calling Dr. Drake . . . emergency in the north birch grove."

"How did you know how?"

"I saw Danny do it once for a doe, and then he showed me in his anatomy book what a deer's bones look like."

They walked back toward the road.

"He would have starved to death, wouldn't he."

"Guess so."

"Man, I've really got talented brothers. I'm sorry I was so mean about, you know, Venus and all."

"Ah, you're a mean miserable twin." He socked her lightly on the shoulder, which meant he liked her. Everything was fine.

When they reached the county roads, the snow was unbroken, without even any tire tracks yet.

"Maybe he went home last night," Cassandra said.

"I thought of that." Paige sat down on the sled to think. "As long as we're out here, I'd like to look a little longer."

"What about Moore's Pond?"

"Well, it's as good a place as any, I guess."

When they came to the road that led to the pond, they turned in.

"I'll take the trail that cuts off to the north, and you go on over to the pond. No sense our both covering the same ground. We'll rendezvous at the dam in thirty minutes, and if we haven't found any trace by then, we'll go home and see if he's there." He looked at his watch. "Let's synchronize our watches."

"Right."

"I have twenty two after seven."

"Check."

He trotted down the narrow road that led through the woods. The sled moved easily on the new snow. At the point where the other trail branched off, he stopped. "I'll take the sled, okay? If you find him, just sit tight and wait for me."

She hated to see him go. As soon as he was out of sight, she had a feeling of intense desolation. The early light filtered dimly through the snowy trees. It was very still but she was sure all sorts of animals and birds were watching her. Not that she didn't love animals and birds and under most circumstances feel at home with them, but in that white silence she couldn't shake off an ominous feeling. She was glad she would probably never go to the North or South

Pole. Although it would be fun to see a bunch of penguins.

She followed the narrow overgrown road to Moore's Pond. Once she had persuaded Poppy to bring the family to the pond for a picnic, and he had lost his usually unloseable temper because the branches had scratched the new station wagon. Once you got a car into the road, there was no way out except to go all the way to the pond and turn around, or back up. It hadn't been their most successful picnic.

Moore's Pond both fascinated and scared her. It was not very wide but it was fairly long, and in the middle it shelved off deeply. There was a dam and a mill wheel from some long ago operation; she had never been able to find out what kind. The story was that two men had come in with some kind of plans and then had simply disappeared. No one knew where they had gone or why. Poppy laughed at the story; he thought they'd just found that whatever they had in mind wasn't practical; but Cassandra was sure it was some kind of mystery. Moore's Pond was a spooky place, all right.

There was a leaky old rowboat that she and Paige sometimes pulled out of the bushes and poled around the pond, bailing like mad to keep it from sinking.

When she got to the pond, she stopped and

looked all around. She whistled and called. If Bingo was near, he would smell her even if she didn't make any noise; Labs had a fabulous sense of smell. Ronald used to take him bird hunting; he said he had a gentle mouth. She was glad he had a gentle mouth.

The pond looked like a big white frosted cake. She went around to the north and climbed up on the dam, moving slowly so as not to slip. She brushed away the snow and sat down. From there she could see a long way. Off to the southwest the woods were interrupted by a meadow where she sometimes picked wild flowers in the spring. It was one of her favorite places.

She hadn't been back to the pond since the family picnic. She remembered that after supper, Danny had built up the fire and they'd sat around it telling stories, the woods dark and scary behind them. Poppy had told a terrifying story about *The Face at the Window.* It turned out all right because what looked like a human head that was scaring everybody in the story turned out to be a porcupine, but she had been so frightened by the story that she shivered again, remembering it. Then Ronald had told *The Monkey's Paw,* and that was even worse. Muth finally called a halt to the gruesome stories, but then Roz had done a little dance along the top of the dam and that had scared Cassandra even more, because there was her real live sister looking like a ghost, dancing in the

68

dark. Poppy made her quit because he was afraid she'd fall in the pond. She wouldn't have, of course. Roz could probably dance with perfect safety on the edge of a saber if she chose to.

Cassandra slid down the broad side of the dam, retraced her steps, and continued on toward the south. Icy bushes snapped and crunched under her boots. She hoped she wasn't trampling on anybody's winter den. She'd hate to tread on some woodchuck's bedroom.

She saw the tracks of a fox, recognizing it by the big sweep in the snow that his tail had made. She knew there were fox dens over in the meadow. You could see them humped up a little.

Animals were nice. She envied Danny the life he planned to live. He'd turned down basketball scholarships from four eastern colleges already because he wanted to go out to Fort Collins, Colorado, to study big-animal veterinary medicine. It sounded like a nice life. She wondered what Paige would really do. Last year he was going to be a chemist, and the year before that a fingerprint expert for the FBI. Now radio stuff because he liked Buddy Baker and his dumb old radio. Well, whatever it was, it would probably take him a long way from her. People said it was so great to be twins, and until lately it had been; but now she felt as if she were being split right down the middle, and

69

it hurt like fury.

She stopped. She thought she heard a bark. She stood holding her breath, listening. There it was again, faint and far off. She cocked her head, trying to tell where it came from. It didn't sound like Bingo's deep voice, but after all, he was hurt and he might sound different. Sometimes if someone accidentally stepped on his toes, he yipped like that.

It came again, and then she was sure it was from the meadow. Bingo must be in the meadow! Oh, if only Paige would hurry back. She wished she had the sled. But she could go and comfort him anyway.

She ran out onto the pond, to take the shortest way to the meadow. Bingo, I'm coming, she kept saying aloud. She was almost in the middle of the pond when she heard the ice crack. In front of her, where the wind had swept the snow away, she saw cracks shoot like lightning across the black ice. Black ice! Only at that moment did she realize that she should have checked out the condition of the ice. There was another louder crack, like a rifle shot, and she felt the ice buckle under her. She tried to jump back, but it was too late. With a cracking, grinding sound the ice gave way beneath her, and she fell into the bitterly cold water.

FIVE

As Cassandra felt herself fall, she grabbed at the edges of ice near her. For a moment she hung on, but then the ice broke and she went into the water up to her shoulders. Frantically she reached again and found ice that would hold.

For a moment she couldn't breathe at all. She felt as if she were encased in tight elastic. The cold and even the wetness didn't penetrate her ski pants for the first few seconds but then she felt the frigid water right through to her skin. She clung to the ice trying to think what to do. If she put too much pressure on the ice, it too would break away. But she had to do something quickly. Sharp pains shot up her legs, and her boots felt like iron weights pulling her down. And then the numbness came. A person could die in water that cold, in seven or eight minutes. Something had to be done.

Cautiously she tried to kick her legs in a scissors kick, but she couldn't really tell that they had even moved. She was shivering so hard, her teeth rattled. She would have to stay calm . . . stay calm, Cass, stay calm. Paige wouldn't be back for twenty minutes at least.

The slow current of the water pulled at her legs. This is what I have to do, she told herself; I have to break the ice a little at a time until I get to a piece strong enough to hold me or until I get to a place where I can touch bottom. It shouldn't be too far; only the middle part of the pond was really deep. Poppy wouldn't let us swim there. So all you have to do, Cassandra, is get to the place where the bottom shelves up. Just that.

Now. Break the ice away a little at a time, and keep your arms spread apart so if one place breaks, the other one may hold. It was going to be tricky, all right. She tried to force herself to stop shivering, but it was impossible. The cold wind whipped at her wet jacket and her bare head. Her hood had fallen back when she went into the water. Letting go of the ice with one hand, she tried to pull the hood back up, but she couldn't button it and in a few seconds the wind caught it and blew it back again.

Very cautiously she moved her right hand along the ice, hit it gently, then harder. She had to hit it several times before it broke off in a chunk about a foot wide. As she lost her support on her right side, she dipped into the water sideways and came up gasping. Her wet glove froze to the ice and had to be jerked loose. The water around her was black and menacing, and

she remembered how she had always felt there was something ominous about Moore's Pond. But that was silly. This was no time for that kind of thinking.

She broke another chunk of ice loose, and the break extended to the spot where she held on with her left hand. She went down over her head.

She surfaced and thrashed, trying to clutch the ice ahead of her. She caught hold, the piece broke, but she had time to grab again at a frozen hummock of grass that stuck out of the ice in front of her.

It seemed as if she had been in the freezing water for hours. She wanted to look back to see if she had made any progress, but she didn't dare turn. She was beginning to lose control of her hands. If she was going to make it, it was now or never. The ice seemed to be thicker there. If she hadn't come out on the pond running, she probably would have fallen in sooner, nearer the shore, maybe right about where she was now. Did that mean she dared try to hoist herself out? She decided to try. If she really exerted herself, she might get out, and also it might help her to keep from freezing.

With a tremendous effort she tried to get herself up onto the ice. She failed, and a narrow ledge broke away. Now she was leaning against the ice, and she didn't think she could move again. "This is it. I'm going to die here." Her hands, now almost useless, lost their hold, and she waited to sink. "Paige," she said aloud.

She wasn't sinking. Very slowly the realization became clear. She wasn't sinking! Because she had lost all feeling in her feet, it had taken her a few seconds to understand that she was standing on the bottom. She had reached shallow water.

"Well, I'm not going to stand here and freeze to death," she said aloud. With an effort that seemed to be pulling up from the very soles of her feet, she tried again to climb out onto the ice. "You've got to do it, Cassandra. Paige will be mad if you just stand here and die in shallow water like a ninny. Get the left leg up. Up, up! Boost with arms. UP!" She floundered, half made it, slid back a little, tried again and made it. She was out.

She tried to get up and run the few feet to shore. The headlong effort took her to the snow and brush at the edge of the pond, but then her legs gave way and she fell into the bushes. There she passed out.

She regained consciousness enough to know that Paige was there, trying to lift her. She wanted to help him but she couldn't move. She flickered out. When she came to again, she was tied to the sled on her stomach, her arms folded under her head. Dimly she could see Paige's legs, in his thin blue jeans, flying up and down as he ran down the road. He had her wet ski

75

pants under an arm and he was wearing her parka, unzipped and flapping behind him.

She closed her eyes again, feeling the jolts as the sled hit ruts in the road. She felt as if she were sliding in and out of time. There was Paige untying the rope and carrying her somewhere. She was too tired to open her eyes. Then she heard him running, close by, then gone, then back. She smelled smoke and heard the crackle of a fire.

She opened her eyes. She was lying on the floor in front of the fire in the recreation building, wrapped in a torn Army blanket, wearing Paige's parka and heavy pants. She felt something warm and hard against her legs. She reached down and found they were rocks, heated rocks. Paige was gently lifting her feet and then she felt warm water.

"Can I get closer to the fire?"

She saw the look of relief lighten his face when she spoke. "Hi. No, we have to warm you up gradually. You've got some frostbite in your feet."

"Is it bad?" Sometimes people lost their feet from frostbite.

"I don't think so. Don't worry. As soon as we get you thawed out, I'll take you home and Dr. Storey will take care of things. Here, see if you can drink this." He held a steaming cup to her face. "It's tea. Drink it as hot as you can. Slow."

It burned her tongue, but she drank it anyway. She could feel the wonderful heat all the way down into her stomach. She'd never known before how great something hot could be. "Oh, that's good!" She was still shivering.

"I'll fix some more."

Her feet were beginning to pain her badly. She told him.

"I know. You remember how that used to happen, a little, when we stayed out tobogganing too long on a cold day?"

"Yes." She clenched her teeth. It really hurt. "Was I there very long, unconscious and all?"

"I don't think so. I came over to the pond soon after I branched off."

"How come you came early?" She wanted to talk so she wouldn't notice the pain so much.

"I don't know. I thought I heard you call me."

"I did, but you couldn't have heard me."

"I didn't hear you with my ears, more like in my head. It was weird."

She tried to smile. "Well, we're twins."

"Yeah." He watched her face. "God, I wish I had some aspirin or something." He exchanged the heated rocks for some warmer ones.

"I'll survive."

"Hey, I wonder if there would be any in the cottage. It's the only place I haven't broken into."

"Don't go away."

"I'll only be a couple minutes. It would help you a lot. I'll be real quick. I'm getting to be a very good second-story man."

She hated to see him go. It was easier to bear the pain when he was there. She drank some more tea as hot as she could stand it, and waited for him to come back. Suddenly it occurred to her that she hadn't even told him about hearing the barking. He'd be wanting to rush out there and rescue Bingo. Then they could all go home and Dr. Storey would fix her feet and her legs. She touched the baggy pants that used to be Ronald's hunting pants. Paige must be cold in just his light jeans. But he never minded the cold as much as the rest of them did. Ronald used to call him "my brother, the Eskimo." She wished he'd hurry back. Of course he'd have to leave again at once; they couldn't leave Bingo out there alone.

He burst in, waving a bottle. "Hey! Got 'em. Anacin. Mrs. Carstairs isn't as tough as she seems." He dumped two tablets into her hand and filled the cup with water from the kettle. "That ought to help."

"I hope so. It's getting kind of rugged." She lay back, holding her hands clenched together. "Paige, I've got to tell you—"

"Just take it easy. Don't talk till you feel better."

"No, I have to. I ran out on the pond because I was trying to get to the meadow. I think Bingo is out there."

He wheeled around to look at her. "Bing?"

"I heard a bark, several times. Three times."

"Bing's bark?" His face was intent. "Bing's, Cass?"

"I couldn't be sure. It was high and yippy, like when we stepped on his paw or something."

He stood holding the kettle, frowning. "It could be a fox."

"Oh." She hadn't thought of the foxes. It could have been. "But it might not. We have to make sure. You go out there now, Paige. I'll be all right here."

For a moment he looked at her. Then he shook his head. "Not till I get you home first. As soon as you're warmed up a little and the pills start to work, I'll take you home on the sled. Then I'll come back and check out the meadow. If Danny's home, he can bring me on the snowmobile."

"He won't use it." Danny hated the noise and destruction of the snowmobile.

"He would for an emergency."

"Please, go now."

He shook his head. "No way."

She felt both relieved and exasperated. She had made the decision that he should go; now he wouldn't do it. "Bingo needs you."

79

"So do you. Twin first." He propped the kettle on a log.

It was years since they'd used that expression. When they were little, they would never go anywhere without each other, or do anything unless the other one wanted to do it, too. "Twin first," they would say, and it became a family saying. Once when Paige had been very sick with the flu, she had spent three days in a chair beside his bed, Muth bringing her her meals. Twin first.

She didn't argue with him. She lay still and willed the Anacin to work, and soon the pains did begin to diminish. "They're going away." She felt drowsy and no longer so anxious.

"Good. Want some more tea?"

"Just a little. I'm practically awash." She drank a little, and fell asleep.

When she woke up, she felt much better. Paige was just changing the water that her feet were soaking in. "Oh, I feel better!"

"Good. You can move closer to the fire if you want to."

"I felt so . . . I don't know . . . worried before. Now I don't." She moved the heated rocks and came up closer to the fire. "Those rocks are a great idea. How'd you know all this stuff?"

"Read Danny's First Aid book." He touched the

lining of her parka that hung near the fire. "These are really good parkas. The top part of you hardly got wet."

She shuddered. "It was awful."

"It must have been real scary. I shouldn't have left you by yourself."

"Don't be silly. I'm not a baby."

"No, but we should have stuck together." He held out the can of peanut butter. "I know it isn't very groovy stuff to eat by itself, but you ought to eat something."

She made herself eat several sticky gobs, and then she finished off last night's popcorn. "Can I try standing up?"

"Sure, but take it easy." He gave her a hand up. Her legs were wobbly, and she felt terribly weak.

"I'm going to pull you on the sled." He was busy putting out the fire.

"You don't have to do that. I can walk."

"Don't argue. I'll come back tomorrow and clean up this place and put the things back."

"What about the thing on the chimney?"

"Oh, no squirrel is going to dive down that chimney between now and morning. It'll be too hot for a while, for one thing. The thing is now to get you home. Do you feel warm?"

"Yes. I'm fine." But by the time he had helped her

81

to the top of steps outside, she was glad to sit down on the sled. She held the coil of rope and her still damp pants, while Paige wrapped the blanket loosely around her legs.

"Well, here we go. Sing out if you're not all right." He set off down the wide path at a steady trot.

SIX

THE WEATHER HAD CLEARED. THE SKY WAS BLUE, THE wind had died down, and the temperature seemed to have risen, or else the warmth of the sun made it seem so. Cassandra felt better than she had expected to. Her legs and feet felt funny, but they didn't hurt.

When they came to the road to Moore's Pond, Cassandra called to Paige to stop.

"What's up? Am I going too fast?"

"No. I want us to go around by the meadow."

He shook his head emphatically. "No. First you go

home. Then I'll come back."

"No, Paige, listen. I feel much better. I've done everything you said, but now it's my turn to say. Please go to the meadow. Bingo may need us right now."

He thought it over. "Well, all right, if you'll promise to stay on the sled, no running around."

"I couldn't run around if I wanted to."

He pushed his hair back from his damp forehead; he was breathing hard from the fast pace he had kept up. "All right. We can kind of loop around and cut back to the road in a half circle. I guess it won't be too much out of the way."

He turned into the pond road. In a few minutes she had to ask him to slow down a little, the road was so bumpy.

When they came to the pond and she saw the jagged patch of black water, she shuddered and closed her eyes. It was very strange to think of having come that close to dying. When she thought about it, she couldn't believe she had done anything so stupid as to run out on the ice at this time of year, without even testing it. With the thaws they'd already had, she should have known it might not hold. It was nice of Paige not to point out how dumb she'd been.

Paige stopped at the southern end of the pond and called Bingo. There was no answering bark. What if he had . . . she couldn't finish the sentence even in her mind. If only she had used her head, she could have rescued him and they'd have had him home and at the vet's already. If anything happened to him, she'd never forgive herself. It would be the end of everything nice.

When they reached the meadow, they both called, Still no answer. Paige pointed to a hump in the earth on the other side of the meadow. "Fox's den. You might have heard a fox. But I'll scout around anyway. You stay here."

She leaned forward tensely on the sled, watching him as he started an orderly check of the meadow. He went halfway around, then cut across diagonally, then back on the other side of the diagonal. She shaded her eyes, trying to see all the places he hadn't come to yet. Muth always said she had sharp eyes.

The sun on the snow was blinding. She closed her eyes for a moment, seeing dark spots dance on the retina. Then she opened them again, squinting, and looked down the length of the meadow where it stretched away from her. Her attention was caught by something dark, lying half in the brush, half in the meadow. She stared at it, not breathing. It was probably a log or something. She looked for Paige, but he was at the far end of the meadow now. She couldn't wait for him to come back. In spite of her promise, she got off the sled and walked toward the dark bulk. Her knees shook and she knew she shouldn't be walking,

but she had to see.

As she came closer, she saw it was an animal of some kind, lying very still. Then she saw that it was Bingo. Afraid to look, afraid not to, she turned and shouted for Paige, who came running. She had reached the dog before Paige caught up with her.

She thought he was dead. His eyes were closed, and he was absolutely still.

"Bingo!" It was too terrible to face. She wanted to lie down in the snow and just blank out. She put her hand on his shoulder. It felt warm. Not daring to believe it (it could mean he hadn't been dead long enough to turn cold), she slid her hand under his chest. There was a faint, unmistakable heartbeat.

She looked up into Paige's face. "He's alive! Paige, he's alive."

Paige knelt beside her and felt the heartbeat for himself. "Just barely," he murmured. There was a long, bloodcaked gouge along the dog's body from the back of the head around to the ribcage. "He's lost an awful lot of blood."

But Cassandra was full of new hope. "We've got to get him home fast, Paige. Got to get him to the vet. He'll be all right." She bent down and kissed Bingo's soft ear. "He's going to be just fine."

She stayed there while Paige ran for the sled. Then while she sat on the sled, Paige gently lifted the limp body of the dog and put it part on her lap, part on the front part of the sled. Cassandra insisted that they use the blanket for Bingo. "I'm not cold any more." But she was dizzy, and she closed her eyes to keep the world from spinning. It would be awful if she should faint or anything, when Paige and Bingo needed her.

Paige started the long loop toward the county road, looking back often to make sure everything was all right. Cassandra clung to the sides of the sled with both hands, willing herself to stay conscious. Bingo's body was heavy in her lap, and her legs began to ache again. Hurry, Paige.

She felt as if she were not only willing herself to stay conscious, but willing Bingo to live. He couldn't die, not after all they'd been through together. If your own beautiful dog could die, then anything could happen. A twin, even, could die. . . . She felt the cold twist in her chest. Nobody is going to die, Cassandra. Everything is going to be just fine. Like Muth says, "Into every life a little rain must fall," but that didn't mean it was going to be a solid wall of water that would drown you. Everything's going to be fine, and we'll be playing ball in the meadow in a week, making the sweet silly sheep gallop around as if they were scared to death when they really aren't. Soon we'll be home.

SEVEN

THEY HAD COME OUT ON THE COUNTY ROAD AT LAST.
Paige stopped and said, "Listen!"

Cassandra tried to listen, but she couldn't hear anything unusual. All her energy was concentrated on
staying on the sled and holding Bingo. But then she
heard what Paige was listening to, the hideous but
now welcome roar of Ronald's snowmobile.

"It must be Danny," Paige said. "Thank God."

The snowmobile came up over a hill and it was
Danny driving. He pulled up to them, shut off the
engine, and got off. His face showed his relief, but he

just said, "Where the hell ya been?"

"Man, am I glad to see you!" Paige said.

Danny bent down and looked at Bingo. "Better get him to the vet."

"We can't take him on the snowmobile," Paige said. "The noise and everything might kill him."

"Right."

Paige helped Cassandra up. "Dan, you take Cass home, will you? I'll take Bingo to the vet on my sled. Cass has to get home right away and see Dr. Storey. She fell in Moore's Pond."

"Oh." Danny put his arm around her and helped her onto the snowmobile. "You take her home, Paige. I'll take Bingo to the vet."

"Well, I thought . . ."

"You look zonked out, yourself. You'd both better get on home. Don't worry, I'll take good care of him. You know how to run this thing, I suppose?"

"Sure."

Danny looped the rope around Bingo's body and covered him with the blanket. "Don't go too fast. You can follow my tracks across the—" He broke off. "What am I telling you for. You know this country as well as I do. Cass, you hold onto Paige, all right?"

"All right," she said faintly. She wrapped her arms around Paige's waist.

"Take it easy."

Paige hesitated, looking back at Bingo.

"Don't worry," Danny said. "I'll get him there fast. But Paige—" Danny glanced at Cassandra and didn't finish his sentence. "See you at the house." He picked up the rope of the sled and started running down the road, the sled sliding easily along behind him.

Cassandra leaned her head against Paige's back so she wouldn't have to look at the blanket-covered dog on the sled. She felt the vibration as Paige started the motor. Then they were off. She knew that in spite of everything, what Paige was probably thinking right now was what a blast it was to drive the snowmobile by himself. She knew he was dying to let it out, but he drove carefully and at a moderate speed across the meadows and through the trails in the woods where Danny had already been, looking for them.

They came into their own property, and Cassandra felt like fainting with relief when she saw the barn. There had been so many moments when she hadn't really expected ever to see the place again. They roared across the field and into the yard, scaring the sheep and sending the chickens in all directions. Muth came running out the back door, Poppy right behind her.

Paige brought the machine to a halt at the back steps and shut off the engine. The silence felt good. Cassandra tried to get off, but she had to wait for Paige to help her up.

"What's the matter?" Muth said.

"Better call Dr. Storey," Paige said. "Cass fell into Moore's Pond. She might have some frostbite." Poppy had already gone inside to call the doctor.

Cassandra tried to smile at her mother; she looked so worried. "I'm all right." She let Paige and Muth help her up the steps. She sat down for a minute in the kitchen. It felt so warm and at home. Then Poppy was there, carrying her upstairs to his and Muth's big bedroom.

Ophelia came out of her room, her hair done up in huge rollers. In the background her transistor radio played rock. "What's wrong? Did you find Bingo?"

"Danny's taken him to Dr. Kenneth. Cass fell in the pond."

Muth turned on the electric blanket and helped Cassandra out of her clothes, and into a pair of Paige's flannel pajamas. Now she was here, in the room she had been dreaming about, with Poppy lighting the fire and Paige running downstairs to watch for the doctor.

"I'm going to heat up some of that cream of potato soup." Muth fixed the pillows for Cassandra.

"Better wait and see what Harlow has to say," Poppy said.

"I know what Harlow Storey will say before he's thought of it himself," Muth said. "He's taken care of us so often. 'Keep her warm, feed her good, give her one of these every three hours; let her sleep.' " She sounded so much like Dr. Storey, Poppy and Ophelia laughed. Cassandra tried to laugh, too, but she didn't make any sound.

Rosalind appeared in the doorway in her white tutu and her ballet shoes, her long red-gold hair falling loose around her shoulders. Cassandra thought she looked like the Sugar Plum Fairy. "Hi," she said softly. "Are you all right?"

Cassandra smiled and gave an almost invisible nod.

"I'm glad you're back." She looked around quickly and Cassandra knew she was looking for Bingo.

"At the vet's," Cassandra said.

"Oh." Rosalind came over to the bed and looked down at her, her expressive eyes full of sympathy. They all loved Bingo.

Cassandra half dozed in the marvelous warmth of the blanket and the heat from the fireplace. She woke up long enough to drink the hot milk Paige brought her. She heard her father say, "Is that the right thing, Paige?" and Paige answering firmly, "It's the right thing, Poppy." It pleased her that her father didn't question Paige's wisdom any further. They were beginning to treat him the way they treated Danny, like someone who knew about things.

Then Dr. Storey was there, examining her legs and feet, taking her temperature, blood pressure, pulse, and listening to Paige's account of what had happened and what he had done.

He pulled the blanket up over Cassandra. "Good work, Paige. You did just right."

"Will she . . . she won't have any trouble, will she?"

Cassandra tensed for the answer. In the back of her mind had lingered terrible words, like amputation.

"She'll be fine. Only thing is, she'll probably be more sensitive to cold after this. I'd say it was a near thing though. Lucky she had you along. Did you find your dog?"

"Yes. Danny's taken him to Dr. Kenneth."

"Hope he'll be all right. Fine dog. Martha, keep that girl in bed and warm. Give her something hot, soup or milk or cocoa or whatever she wants, every three or four hours. Plenty of rest. One of these capsules every three hours, and if she has any more pain, give her aspirin. I'll look in on her in the morning. What the devil are you grinning at, Coffey?"

"Just a little family joke, Harlow," Poppy said.

"At my expense, no doubt. Well, I've got a tough hide." He put his instruments back into the little bag.

"It's an affectionate joke, Harlow," Muth said. "You know we love you."

"Ah, Martha, you and your blarney. See you in the morning then. And I'd suggest you get that boy to take a long nap, too. He's tuckered out. Feed him up good."

When he was outside her room, Cassandra heard him say, "Rosalind, you look more like a little princess every day."

Rosalind laughed and said, "Is that a compliment, Dr. Storey?"

"Darned right it's a compliment. We need more pretty little princesses in this dreary world. But I don't want you spending all your time on that dance stuff, Rosalind. Get some fresh air. Are you eating right?"

"I eat like a horse. Ask Muth."

"She does, Harlow."

"Good, good. I can tell *you're* eating all right, Ophelia."

Ophelia giggled. "Dr. Storey! You're a brute!"

"Not a bit, not a bit. I like a healthy girl. You look fine." His voice trailed away as he went down the stairs. Cassandra heard the front door close and then his car starting up.

Paige was sitting near her bed. "Hey," he said, "how about that? I saved your life! Maybe I'll be a doctor."

She knew he was teasing, but it sounded like a good idea. "Great," she said. She was beginning to feel a little better. "You can be Dr. Storey's assistant and some day take over his practice. . . ."

"Nah, not that kind of a doctor. I'd go to the South American jungle or someplace."

There he goes again, she thought. But she was too sleepy and glad to be home to worry about anything. She wanted to tell him to go see how Bingo was; she knew he wanted to. But before she could say it, she fell asleep.

When she opened her eyes again, Paige was asleep in the chair by the fire, his feet in his red mukluks propped up on the ottoman with the needlepoint that Muth had just finished. He looked tired and pale; he ought to be in bed. She was touched that he had stayed here with her.

As she watched him, he stirred and she realized that he was not really asleep. He turned his head a little, and the firelight made him look different. In that moment, his face unguarded, he looked to Cassandra as if he had already grown up; a look of . . . what was it, exactly? . . . sadness and knowledge, something very remote. He was a person she didn't know at all. It frightened her, and she spoke his name.

Instantly he turned toward her, his face taking on its usual look, half kidding, half reserved. It was the first time she had ever seen for herself that he kept part of himself hidden from her.

"How do you feel?" he said.

"Much better."

Ophelia looked in and said, "Oh, you're awake. Muth has some food for you." She disappeared again.

"Aren't you supposed to be resting too?" Cassandra asked him.

"I've been snoozing here."

"Have you heard from Danny?"

"Oh, yeah."

"How's Bing?"

He looked away. "Kind of touch and go, Dr. Kenneth said. Danny's still over there."

"You go over there, too, Paige. I'm all right."

97

He nodded. "Pretty quick."

"Now." She knew he was staying just for her. "I'm practically all recovered."

Ophelia appeared in the door carrying a tray with a bowl of Muth's homemade cream of potato soup made from the potatoes she'd grown last summer, and a big mug of hot chocolate with whipped cream from Mrs. Ames's cow, Dora.

She stopped at the foot of the bed, waiting for Paige to put his feet down so she could get by. "Move, can't you?" she said impatiently.

"Oh." He lowered his feet to the floor and pushed his chair back.

He looked so tired, Cassandra could hardly stand it. "Don't yell at him like that," she said angrily. "He's tired."

"I had to get by, didn't I? I can't just stand here—"

"You could come around the other side of the bed."

Ophelia was hurt. "Man! You try to do something for somebody and what do you get? Yelled at. Next time get your own damned soup."

"Cool it," Paige said.

"Don't you tell me to cool it." She put the tray down with a thump on the bedside table, spilling a little of the hot chocolate. "That's the thanks you get around here."

"I thank you," Cassandra said stiffly. "Just don't

yell at Paige. He's just as worn out as I am. None of you seem to realize that he saved my life. He's a hero."

"Cassandra," Paige said, "shut up and eat your soup."

"What's going on here?" It was Muth at the door. "I just—" Ophelia broke off. "Oh, honestly! Deliver me from having to put up with twins." She swished out of the room, the long skirt of her housecoat billowing behind her.

"You hurt her feelings," Paige said.

"I was only trying to protect you."

He made a face. "Don't bother."

"Here, here," Muth said. "Calm down now. You're both tired; you've been under a great strain. Nobody meant to hurt anybody, I'm sure. Paige dear, I wish you'd go to bed."

"I'm all right. I had a nap."

"Did you eat?" Cassandra asked him.

"Ask Muth. The cupboard is bare. All except the peanut butter."

Muth smiled and put her hand on the back of his neck. "He did just fine."

Danny appeared in the doorway, and both the twins stiffened, afraid of what he might say. He shook his head. "No change. I had to leave. I've got a game."

Paige got up. "I'll go over."

"All right. Don't stay too long, though, Paige. I

99

don't think Kenneth is too hot for having us there. Bing is unconscious. Kenneth is doing everything he can."

The telephone rang, and Cassandra heard Ophelia answer it.

"I want to go, though," Paige said. "I want to see how he is."

"Paige, phone," Ophelia called.

"I'll take it up here," he called back to her. He went out to the hall extension. Cassandra held her breath, afraid it was Dr. Kenneth.

But Paige was saying, "Oh, hi, Buddy. . . . Yeah, our dog got hit by a car. We had to go look for him. . . . He's at the vet's. . . . Don't know yet. I'm going over there now. . . . Well, I could come over tomorrow."

"How can he talk about going anywhere," Cassandra said, "when Bingo is so sick. . . ."

Danny looked at her sympathetically but he didn't say anything.

"Yeah? What kind of equipment?" Paige said, on the phone. "Man, that sounds neat. Maybe we can get Alaska or some place like that. Wouldn't that be a blast? . . . Well, if everything's okay, I'll be over tomorrow after lunch. . . . Right. So long." He hung up and came back into the room. "That was Buddy."

"We know," Cassandra said. "I should think if you

were going to go be with Bingo, you'd get going."

"Well, I had to answer my phone call, didn't I?"

"Not necessarily," she said. "Not necessarily at all. You could have mentioned you had an emergency."

Paige gave her a long, baffled stare. "Oh, bull," he said. He went down the hall and in a minute she heard him run down the stairs and slam the front door.

"Well, I gotta push off," Danny said.

"Shoot lovely baskets, dear," Muth said.

"Thanks for taking care of Bingo, Danny," Cassandra said.

He stretched his long arms pretending to shoot a basket. "No sweat."

"He'll be all right, won't he?" She wished she hadn't asked it as soon as she heard herself speak the words. Danny looked at her uneasily and then looked away.

"I don't know, Cass. He's hurt pretty bad. Kenneth said there was internal bleeding."

"Well, Dr. Kenneth doesn't know everything. I mean he could be wrong."

"Sure he could. Well, see you later."

"Paige should have gone over to the vet's before," Cassandra said, after Danny had gone.

"He wanted to stay with you," Muth said. She was sitting near the fire, knitting. Her needles clicked pleasantly. "He was worried about you."

"What's to worry about? I got kind of chilled, that's

all. I mean he didn't have a *duty* to stay with me."

"I don't think he thought of it as a duty."

Cassandra pulled the pillow over her ears. He did, too; he thought it was his duty. Just a sense of duty because she had stayed with him that time when he had the flu. Well, if all it amounted to was duty, then the hell with it. *The hell with it.*

After a while, Muth said, "Paige looks tired, doesn't he."

"He didn't *sound* tired, when he was talking to Buddy." She turned over and punched the pillow. "It doesn't seem to have occurred to him that Bingo might . . . Bingo might need him tomorrow."

Muth looked at her for a moment. "I think it's occurred to him." She held up her knitting to the light to check a stitch. "You two have always been so close."

"Have been," Cassandra muttered.

In a minute Muth put down her knitting and came to sit on the foot of Cassandra's bed. "Cassandra dear, you're going through a difficult time. I've watched you and wished I could help you, but I suppose we all have to go through these things alone."

In one of the bewildering quick changes that hit her so often lately, her mood went from resentment to remorse. "Why don't you just say I'm acting like a spoiled brat," she said, "because that's what I'm doing."

"You're not a spoiled child. You're a good child . . . and I'm going to have to stop saying 'child' pretty soon, I guess. You're a good person. But . . ." she spread her hands. "I guess growing up is twice as hard for twins, especially if they're as close as you and Paige have been. But, Cass . . ." she reached out and smoothed the pillow case. "You and Paige are growing into two quite different people, each of you developing his own interests and friends. I think Paige made the break . . . no, 'break' isn't the right word . . . Paige struck out on his own first. It could have been the other way around, but it happened to be this way. And you feel left out."

Cassandra lay still, listening almost without breathing. It frightened her to hear all this.

"And if that didn't happen to you, your lives would be terribly narrow. If you confined yourselves to each other, don't you see, Cassandra? It wouldn't do at all. You'd tie each other down instead of helping each other to richer lives. You'll never really lose Paige, and he won't lose you, unless one of you tries too hard to hang on."

"Well, that sounds true," Cassandra said, "but just supposing he takes off for some place, like the South

American jungle. What do I do then?"

Muth sighed. "Well, honey, I guess you'll do what we all do. Keep on loving him and wish him well."

Cassandra looked at her mother's head and noticed that the chestnut brown hair was getting grayer on top. All of a sudden it struck her that parents had to go through what she was going through, over and over, with every child they had. "I'm never going to have any children," she said.

Muth's expression changed. "I don't want ever to hear you say a thing like that again. Life is full of pain and parting, Cassandra, and you may as well find that out now. You're not going to be exempt. But it's also full of great joy and love. Life is to be lived, and if my children haven't learned that, I'm a miserable failure as a mother."

Cassandra leaned forward and put her arms around her mother. "No, you're not. You're the greatest mother there is. And I'm never going to leave you. I'm going to stay right here and look after you and Poppy forever."

Gently Muth disengaged Cassandra's arms. "Don't you see, that would make us very unhappy?"

Cassandra couldn't believe her ears. "Unhappy to have me here? I thought you liked me."

Muth shook her head helplessly. "Cass, Cass. Well,

I guess it has to be learned; it can't be told. Dear, we love you very much and we love having you here now, but when you are grown, the happiness will come from seeing you blossom out, like a . . ."

"Like a flower?"

"Exactly. We will be so excited, seeing all the wonderful things you do, hearing about what happens to you, who you meet and everything."

"I'll call you every week long distance," Cassandra said. "Weekend rates."

Muth laughed. "We'll be sitting by the phone."

"No, you won't," Cassandra said. "You'll be out helping a lamb to get born, and Poppy will be making a new antique. That's what you mean, isn't it. About things keeping on going."

"Yes. That's it, I guess."

"Well . . ." Cassandra leaned forward till she could see her own face in the mirror over the fireplace. Did she look any older? Sadder but wiser? As far as she could tell, there'd been no change. "I'll think about what you said. I really will."

Muth leaned over and kissed her cheek. "I'm going down to get you something to eat. Would you like melted cheese on toast?"

"Yes. Good."

After Muth had gone, Cassandra lay back and tried

to let it all sink in. She imagined Paige as a famous doctor, like Dr. Schweitzer, saving lives in the jungle. She would read about it in the paper and see him on TV. He'd have a memorial stamp dedicated to him, and she might write his biography. She would say to people, very casually, "That's my twin, you know." Or if he picked up some staggering message from Venus . . . "That's my twin. Oh yes, he was always interested in that kind of stuff. I remember when we were young, he had this friend with a short wave radio and . . ." and she could tell her children about their Uncle Paige. He'd always try to spend Christmas with them, and finally he'd manage to get there, wearing a beard and a trench coat and driving a Land Rover. Or she might herself be a famous actress by that time, and she would call him onstage to take a curtain call with her. "Ladies and gentlemen," she'd say, giving them her famous gracious smile, "I want to present to you that great and justly famous man, my twin, Dr. Paige Drake." She closed her eyes and smiled, hearing the thunderous applause. Then they'd rush off to a special midnight recital that Roz was giving in Carnegie Hall, and after that they'd spend Christmas with Ophelia and her executive husband and their beautiful children. Danny would fly in from an important wildlife conference in the West; Ronald, from skiing

in the Alps; and Muth and Poppy would come from
New Hampshire, and it would be just the darnedest
best Christmas they'd ever had.

EIGHT

CASSANDRA WAS NOT AWAKE WHEN PAIGE GOT HOME from the vet's, but when she woke up in the middle of the night, he was asleep in the chair by the bed. She reached out and touched his arm. "Paige . . ." she said softly. "Paige, wake up and go to bed. I'm all right now."

He sat up with a jerk, looking for a moment as if he didn't know where he was. "Oh," he said. "Hi."

"Hi. Go to bed. Thanks for sitting up with me, but

I'm fine now."

He hesitated. "I wanted to tell you something."

"What is it?"

He got out of the chair and hunched down beside the bed. "Cassandra . . ." his voice was so low, she could hardly hear him.

"What is it?"

"Bingo is dead."

"Oh!" In spite of everything, she hadn't expected it. It simply hadn't seemed like something that could happen. "Paige, were you there when . . . when he died?"

"Yeah." He put his face on the pillow. "He just never woke up."

"He wasn't in pain then."

"Not then." His shoulders began to shake, and Cassandra realized he was crying, although he made no sound.

She put her arm around his neck and hugged him hard. There was nothing to say that would do any good. Even when he was a little boy, Paige never cried unless he was hurt beyond endurance.

After a minute he loosened her arm and stood up. "We don't even know who did it." He wiped his face with the sleeve of his sweatshirt.

"It wouldn't make any difference."

"It would to me. I'd pound hell out of him. He'd

never hit another dog when I got through with him."
He pulled out his handkerchief and blew his nose.
"Muth didn't want me to wake you up, but I thought
you ought to know."

"Oh, yes. Thank you."

He took a long shaky breath. "Well, see you in the
morning."

"Try not to feel too bad, Paige."

"How can I not feel bad?"

"Well, I know. I just mean . . . I guess these things
happen. It's the way life is, or something."

"Somebody ought to be able to think of a better
system." He lifted his hand, and went out of the room,
a pale shadow in his light blue pajamas. She saw his
face for a second as he passed the night light in the
hall, and then he was gone.

Cassandra lay back on the pillow and cried quietly
for a long time. Something had ended.

In the morning when Muth brought her breakfast,
she said, very quietly, "Cassandra, they all want me
to tell you how sorry we are, how bad we feel." She put
down the tray and kissed Cassandra's forehead.

"I know," Cassandra said. "Thank you. Can't I get
up?"

"Wait till the doctor comes. I imagine he'll let you
up then."

"All right." She found a note from Rosalind on her tray. "Dear Cassandra: As you know, I have started doing some choreography of my own. Because you and Paige and Bingo always seemed like something very special to me, I would like to title my new dance 'Loyalty: for Bingo and the Twins.' Love, Rosalind." She folded it carefully and put it in her pajama pocket to show Paige later.

When Muth was gone, she ate a little breakfast and then just sat still, listening to the sounds of the house. The clatter of breakfast dishes downstairs; Poppy's deep rumbly voice; the smack of the Sunday paper as it hit the front door, and the door opening as Poppy or Danny got it; Ophelia's little radio giving the news, and the weather from Block Island to Sandy Hook, "a warming trend . . . wind out of the south at ten miles an hour"; the sound of someone, probably Paige, taking a shower. Outside, a rooster was still crowing, as if he couldn't get over it that day had come again. A peacock screamed, and the bell that the old ewe wore tinkled. Sunshine filtered through the muslin curtains with their ball fringe, and made a pattern on the hardwood floor and on the braided rug beside the bed. It felt like spring.

Later Ophelia brought her radio for Cassandra to use, and Danny came in, carrying the box with the fox kits. He called Paige into the room.

"I thought maybe you and Cass would look after the kits for me. They ought to be fed every few hours, and I'm off at practice so much." He put the box on the floor beside the bed.

"Sure." Paige knelt beside them and touched one of the fluffy balls of fur. "We'll take care of them. Can they go from before school till lunch without a meal?"

"Yeah. They're used to that now. They'll have to be turned loose, though, when they're big enough.

All right?" He looked at Paige.

"Sure. Naturally."

Muth and Poppy came into the room, Poppy bringing Cassandra the comic section.

"Dan," Paige said, "can you go up to the camp with me for an hour or so? I've got to clean the place up. If you can't make it, I can go alone."

"I'll go."

"Clean up what?" Poppy said.

"Well, I broke into the rec building, and we built a fire, and opened some food, and used up the firewood; and I broke into the Inn and the Cottage . . . I jimmeyed some of the locks. . . ."

"My God," Poppy said, "I've raised a vandal."

"Let's be glad we raised an efficient vandal," Muth said contentedly. She was rewinding a ball of scarlet yarn.

"We could go on the snowmobile . . ." Paige said, looking at Danny.

"Oh, no, we won't. We'll walk. No more damned snowmobile. They scare hell out of the animals."

"You don't have basketball practice today, do you?" Poppy said.

"Afraid so." He grinned. 'You know the public school system, shot through with atheism."

"I know. Team, town, and God, in that order."

"Don't be blasphemous, Coffey," Muth said, biting

off a piece of yarn.

"Only staying with the trend. A teacher has to be a very trendy fellow. We've got to beat North Conway, or what's a heaven for?"

"What are you going to do this afternoon, Paige?" Muth said.

Paige glanced at Cassandra and then looked away. "I don't know. Nothing special."

She knew what was in his mind. He wanted to go to Buddy's, but he hesitated to say so because he didn't want to upset her. After he left the room, she stopped listening to what the others were talking about.

In a few minutes she put on her slippers and robe and went down to Page's room. He was lying on his bed staring at the ceiling.

"Hi," she said, which was a dumb thing to say when she had just been talking to him.

"Hi."

"I wanted to say, if you wanted to go over to Buddy's and see his new equipment and all, I could go out to camp with Danny and show him what has to be done."

He looked at her suspiciously. "Why are you saying that?"

"Because I mean it."

"You can't get out of bed."

"I can when Dr. Storey comes. We could drive out

to the lake in Danny's jalopy."

He studied her. "No, I'll go."

"Then you could go to Buddy's this afternoon."

"Why are you so fired up about my going to Buddy's?"

"I just think it would do you good. Take your mind off things. If you feel like going to see your friend, you should go."

He sat up. "Did Muth tell you to say that?"

"Paige!"

"Well, it doesn't sound like you."

She had to struggle to keep her new, calm, grown-up tone. "We're growing up, that's all. We can't hang onto each other like little babies. You'll have your friends. I'll have mine."

He looked at her for quite a while. "On the level?"

"On the level."

He nodded. "All right. Fine." He got up and began to comb his hair. "Thanks, Cass."

She looked at his face in the mirror, at her own face beside it. They didn't look as much alike as they used to, she thought. His face was getting longer or something. "Don't forget the cap on the chimney."

"I won't."

As she went out of the room, she noticed Bingo's collar on top of Paige's bureau. She felt something like a hard dry place in her chest, and she thought, "so that's how grief feels."

She walked slowly back down the hall. Her feet felt all right today. She was as good as new. How good was new, though? Well, she had done what you're supposed to do; she had taken a step down the road that said "for adults only"; and in her opinion, it wasn't all that great.

Only her mother was still in her room. She looked up and smiled at Cassandra. "I don't know why I'm sitting here winding up a ball of yarn, with all there is to do."

But Cassandra knew why she had come, why they had all come, to try and cheer up the twins. She got into bed, although she was getting pretty bored with bed. "Do you think I'd be any good as an actress?"

"I think you might. Would you like to try it?"

"Well, I've got to do something."

Muth finished the ball of yarn and put it on the table. "Perhaps when Olive and Bill Harris open their summer theater at Tamworth, they could use you on the crew."

"Crew?" She had been thinking in terms of leading roles.

"You have to learn the ropes; acting is a serious profession. Being on the crew, you watch rehearsals a lot and you see how the professionals do it. It's the same as it would be if Paige decides to be a doctor; he would spend years learning how, being a student and then an apprentice, so to speak."

"Like passing the scalpel, and all that?"

"Something like that."

"What does a person do on the crew?"

"Before I was married, I was properties mistress at a theater in Maine."

Cassandra stared at her in astonishment. "Did you want to act?"

"Oh, I thought about it."

"You never told us."

"I met Poppy and forgot all about it."

Cassandra considered this amazing news. "I'll never give up the theater for any man."

Muth bent her head, and Cassandra thought she saw a shadow of a smile, but it was gone when Muth looked at her again.

"Will you write Mrs. Harris and ask her?"

"No, I think you should."

"Can I use your good stationery?"

"Yes. You might ask her about acting classes. I think they started that a year or two ago."

"Wow!" Cassandra sat bolt upright. "I'm going to be an actress. Wait till I tell Paige!"